Here's what kids and grown-ups have to say about the Magic Tree House® books:

"Oh, man . . . the Magic Tree House series is really exciting!"
—Christina

"I like the Magic Tree House series. I stay up all night reading them. Even on school nights!"
—Peter

"Jack and Annie have opened a door to a world of literacy that I know will continue throughout the lives of my students."
—Deborah H.

"As a librarian, I have seen many happy young readers coming into the library to check out the next Magic Tree House book in the series."
—Lynne H.

Magic Tree House®

For a list of Magic Tree House® Merlin Missions and other Magic Tree House titles, visit MagicTreeHouse.com.

MAGIC TREE HOUSE®

#29 A BIG DAY FOR BASEBALL

BY MARY POPE OSBORNE

COVER ILLUSTRATION BY SAL MURDOCCA
INTERIOR ILLUSTRATIONS BY AG FORD

A STEPPING STONE BOOK™

Random House 🏠 New York

To Jenna Lettice and her family

Text copyright © 2017 by Mary Pope Osborne
Cover art copyright © 2017 by Sal Murdocca
Interior illustrations copyright © 2017 by AG Ford

Visit us on the Web!
rhcbooks.com
MagicTreeHouse.com

Educators and librarians, for a variety of teaching tools, visit us at
RHTeachersLibrarians.com

Library of Congress Cataloging-in-Publication Data is available upon request.
ISBN 978-1-5247-1308-9 (trade) — ISBN 978-1-5247-1309-6 (lib. bdg.) —
ISBN 978-1-5247-1310-2 (ebook) — ISBN 978-1-5247-1311-9 (pbk.)

Printed in the United States of America
10 9 8 7 6 5 4 3 2 1

This book has been officially leveled by using the F&P Text Level Gradient™ Leveling System.

CONTENTS

PROLOGUE

One summer day in Frog Creek, Pennsylvania, a mysterious tree house appeared in the woods. It was filled with books. A boy named Jack and his sister, Annie, found the tree house and soon discovered that it was magic. They could go to any time and place in history just by pointing to a picture in one of the books. While they were gone, no time at all passed back in Frog Creek.

Jack and Annie eventually found out that the tree house belonged to Morgan le Fay, a magical librarian from the legendary realm of

Camelot. Since then, they have traveled on many adventures in the magic tree house and completed many missions for Morgan.

Now Jack and Annie are about to find out what their next magic tree house mission will be!

1

FLY BALL

The early Saturday-morning air was damp and chilly. Jack sat on his front porch steps. His chin was cupped in his hands.

Annie came out the front door.

"Do you want Mom to take us to the rec center now?" she asked. It was the day for baseball tryouts.

"I've decided not to go," said Jack.

Annie sat down next to him. "What's wrong?" she asked.

"I can't stop thinking about last season's

3

tryouts," said Jack. "I fell down when I swung the bat. Everybody laughed."

"Yeah, well, everybody laughed at me, too," said Annie. "Remember, I threw the ball to the wrong team."

"So maybe neither of us should go," said Jack.

"But our whole family *loves* baseball," said Annie. "We read about it. We watch it. We learn batting averages. We—"

Before Annie could finish, something dropped from the sky and rolled across their front yard.

"What's that?" said Jack. He and Annie ran down the steps.

A small white ball lay in the grass. Annie grabbed it.

"It's a baseball!" she said.

"Where did it come from?" said Jack.

He and Annie walked to the sidewalk and looked up and down their street. No one was there.

"Maybe it's from another world," whispered Annie. She handed the ball to Jack.

"That's crazy," said Jack. "What other world?"

4

"Think about it," said Annie. "One second, we're talking about baseball—and how we don't want to go to tryouts. The next, this baseball drops from the sky!"

"Oh. You mean—" said Jack.

"Morgan!" Jack and Annie said together.

Annie took off down the sidewalk. "Let's go!" she called to Jack.

"Hold on!" Jack shouted. He put the mysterious ball inside his backpack and raced after Annie.

Jack and Annie crossed the street and dashed into the Frog Creek woods. They hurried between the trees until they came to the tallest oak.

The magic tree house was back.

"Yay, team!" said Annie. She grabbed the rope ladder and climbed up. Jack followed her into the tree house.

Leaf shadows danced on the wooden floor. Two gray baseball caps sat in the dappled light.

Next to the caps was a book: HISTORY OF BASE-BALL. A red leather bookmark was sticking out from the pages.

Jack picked up the book and opened to the bookmark. The page showed a photo of a baseball stadium. The caption beneath it said:

EBBETS FIELD,

BROOKLYN, NEW YORK,

APRIL 15, 1947

"Ebbets Field?" said Jack. "I've heard of that. It was a famous ballpark."

"Look, there's a message on the bookmark," said Annie.

Jack held the bookmark up to the light.

"It's Morgan's handwriting!" he said. He read aloud:

'Twas a big day for baseball
So many years ago.
Journey to Ebbets Field
To learn what you should know.

"Learn what we should know?" repeated Jack. "To become better ballplayers?"

"Sounds like it!" said Annie. "Morgan must have known about the tryouts." She read the next verse:

These caps are magic
Made only for you
To give you the skill
To know what to do.

"Oh, man, it sounds like these caps will make us great players!" said Jack.

"Yay!" said Annie. She read on:

As long as you wear them
All others will see
The skillful people
You're pretending to be.

"I get it! Everyone else will see us as great players!" said Annie.

"In a Little League game?" said Jack.

"Why not?" said Annie. "Little League teams must have played at Ebbets Field, too."

"Yeah, probably all kinds of teams played there," said Jack.

Annie read more:

When you hear the final score,
Give the ball with the name
To the one who knows best
The rules of the game.

"Our baseball has a name?" said Jack. He pulled the ball out of his pack and turned it over in his hands. "No name here."

"Well, maybe we're supposed to give it one," said Annie. "How about Ballee?"

"Ballee?" said Jack. "I don't think so."

"Okay, okay. How about Fly Ball?" said Annie. "It flew down to us."

"Fine, whatever," said Jack. He put Fly Ball back into his pack. "Ready?"

"Yes! This is going to be so much fun," said Annie.

Jack pointed at the photo of Brooklyn, New York. "I wish we could go there!" he said.

The wind started to blow.

The tree house started to spin.

It spun faster and faster.

Then everything was still.

Absolutely still.

2

OPENING DAY

A spring breeze blew into the tree house. The sky was cloudy.

"Hey, baseball uniforms!" said Annie.

Their clothes had magically changed. They were wearing baseball shoes, long socks, and baggy gray pants. Jack's backpack had turned into a leather bag.

"Look at that!" said Annie. She pointed at the word *batboy* stitched on the front of their jerseys.

"Oh. So we're going to be great *batboys*," said Jack with a frown, "not great *players*."

"Don't worry," said Annie. "I'm sure Morgan thinks that being great batboys will help us become great players."

"But *you* can't be a bat*boy*," said Jack, "and there was no such thing as a bat*girl* back then."

"Don't worry," said Annie. "If we wear these caps, everyone will see what we're pretending to be. Remember?"

"Oh, right . . . ," said Jack.

Annie and Jack picked up their caps and put them on.

"Wow!" Annie said with a big grin.

"Yeah . . . WOW!" said Jack. He felt a surge of excitement and confidence. "I feel like I know everything about baseball now!"

"Me too!" said Annie.

"I can't wait to get to Ebbets Field!" said Jack. "Let's go!" He shoved the baseball book into his backpack. Then he led the way down the rope ladder.

Jack and Annie stepped onto the ground. They'd landed in a small grove of trees. Nearby were stone benches and a fountain. Children were playing on the grass and walkways.

"Looks like a city park," said Jack.

"Let's ask directions," said Annie.

As they headed toward the kids, a gust of wind blew through the park.

"Watch out!" said Jack, grabbing his cap.

Annie held on to her cap, too.

"We can't lose these!" she said.

"No kidding!" said Jack.

They passed a man playing guitar and singing in Spanish. They passed some girls playing jacks. They passed a group of noisy kids shooting marbles.

"Hey, two batboys!" one of the kids shouted.

The others looked up and waved at Jack and Annie.

Annie smiled at Jack. "See? They think I'm a boy," she said. "The magic's working."

"Cool," Jack said with a grin. "You look the same to me, though."

"And you look the same to me," said Annie.

"Maybe we always look like our true selves to each other."

Annie turned back to the kids playing marbles. "Excuse me, how do we get to Ebbets Field?" she called.

"That way!" shouted one of the bigger kids. He pointed across the park. "When you get to the street, it's just a few blocks east."

"You'd better hurry!" yelled a small girl. "The game starts at two-thirty!"

"What time is it now?" Jack called.

One of the boys looked at his watch. "It's one-thirty!" he shouted.

"Oh, man, we're late!" said Jack. "We should've been there at one o'clock to start our chores! Run!"

"Fast!" said Annie. She and Jack held on to their caps and they began running across the windy park.

"Batboys! Batboys! Wait for us!" someone shouted.

Jack and Annie looked back.

The two smallest kids from the marbles game were scrambling after them. Jack thought the boy and girl looked about six years old.

"Sorry! We have to hurry!" Jack yelled.

"But we can help you!" the girl said. "We know a shortcut!"

"You do?" said Annie.

"Yes!" said the boy. "We go to Ebbets Field a lot! This way!"

The small kids turned and started down a dirt path. Annie and Jack ran after them.

"What are your names?" the girl called.

"Jack and—*Andy*!" Annie yelled back. "What's yours?"

"I'm Olive!" said the girl. "This is my twin brother, Otis!"

"Twins? Cool!" said Annie.

"It's a big day for baseball!" said Otis.

"That's what we hear," said Jack.

"I wish we could be batboys like you!" said Otis.

"We know all the rules!" said Olive.

16

The twins led the way to a busy street at the edge of the park. Old-fashioned cars rattled down the broad avenue. The huge cars had long rounded hoods and lots of shiny silver chrome.

Alongside the cars, a trolley clattered over tracks.

Jack and Annie stood at the corner with the twins and waited for the light to change. Nearby, a newsstand was selling the *Brooklyn Eagle*. Jack read a headline:

OPENING DAY AT EBBETS FIELD
BROOKLYN DODGERS VS. BOSTON BRAVES

"Annie, look!" he said, pointing at the newspaper. "We'll be working at a *big-league* game!"

"*Big-league*? Wow!" said Annie.

"You didn't know that?" said Olive.

"I thought the Braves were from Atlanta," Annie said to Jack. "And the Dodgers from L.A.!"

"Not in 1947!" said Jack.

"You didn't know that?" asked Otis.

"Light's red! Let's go!" yelled Jack.

"Hold hands!" cried Olive. She grabbed Annie's hand, and Otis grabbed Jack's. "Watch out for the trolley!"

Jack and Annie ran with the twins across the avenue to the opposite corner.

"Good job!" said Otis.

"Where now?" Jack asked breathlessly.

"We'll take you!" said Olive. "Run!"

"Thanks!" said Jack. He liked the friendly kids.

Jack and Annie held on to their caps as they ran against the wind. They followed Otis and Olive down one street, then another.

"Turn at the corner!" said Olive.

They all turned onto a busy, crowded street.

"There!" the twins said together.

In front of them was the tall brick wall of a stadium. The words EBBETS FIELD curved around the wall. A huge crowd was headed inside.

"Yay!" said Annie, panting. "Thanks for showing us a shortcut, guys!"

"We're not there yet! Come on!" said Olive.

"It's a big day for baseball!" said Otis again. "A really big day!"

3

TAKE ME OUT TO THE BALL GAME

The twins led Jack and Annie to the entrance of the stadium. They all joined the crowd streaming into a huge round lobby. The room had marble walls and a ceiling lamp made of baseball bats.

A sign over the ticket windows said:

$1 GENERAL ADMISSION

"Uh-oh," said Jack. He and Annie reached into the pockets of their uniforms.

"We don't have money," said Annie.

"We don't, either," said Otis. "But we don't need it because—"

"Batboys!" A tall man in a uniform rushed over to them. His badge said SECURITY GUARD.

"That's us," said Jack.

"You're late!" said the guard. "The manager of the visitors' clubhouse is looking everywhere for you! Get over there!"

"Yes, sir!" Jack knew just what the guard meant. The visitors' clubhouse was the place in the stadium where the out-of-town team prepared for the game.

"Wait, can our two friends come watch the game for free?" said Annie. "They helped us—"

"Of course not!" said the guard. "Everyone has to pay—unless they're part of the game. Come on." The guard headed to a turnstile.

"Sorry we can't help you," Jack said to the twins.

"Don't worry. We always watch from Bedford Avenue," Otis said. "We lie on the sidewalk—"

"And peek under a gate," Olive whispered.

"We can see most of center field from there," said Otis. "And a little bit of left field."

"Hey! Batboys!" the guard shouted.

"Gotta go," said Jack. "Thanks a lot!"

"Yeah, thanks a million!" said Annie.

She and Jack hurried through the turnstile and followed the guard. Then they crossed a ramp and headed into the ballpark.

"You're working for the Braves," the guard said. "I'll get the clubhouse manager. Wait here." And he walked away.

"Oh, man," Jack breathed as he and Annie looked around. Compared to the Little League ballpark back home, Ebbets Field was huge.

Fans were filling the stands. A band was playing "Take Me Out to the Ball Game." The breezy air smelled of roasting peanuts, hot dogs, and grilled onions. On the field, umpires in dark suits were talking to each other.

Around the baseball diamond, team members were playing catch. The men all wore jerseys with blue letters that spelled DODGERS.

"Look at the Dodgers batboys," said Annie. "They're helping their team warm up."

"Those batboys look *twice* our age," said Jack.

"I know," said Annie. "But our caps must make everyone see us as teenagers, too."

"That's so incredible," said Jack, smiling. He loved looking older. He loved working for a big-league game. He loved the sights, sounds, and smells of Ebbets Field.

"The fans are really dressed up," said Annie.

In the stands, the men and boys wore suits and hats. The women and girls wore dresses, jackets, and white gloves. It was really different from Frog Creek. At the ballpark at home, grown-ups and kids wore jeans, shorts, and sweatpants.

Jack noticed something else that was different from Frog Creek. Here, half the stands were filling up with mostly white people. The other half were filling up with mostly black people. At home, people of all colors sat together.

Annie pointed to a black Dodgers player signing autographs on baseballs. "Who's *he*?" she said.

Black fans were shouting and waving at the player. Reporters were trying to interview him. A photographer was taking pictures.

"I don't know. He must be a big star," said Jack.

"Hey, batboys! You're late!" someone shouted.

Jack and Annie whirled around.

A short, wiry man was striding toward them. *He must be the manager of the visitors' clubhouse,* Jack thought.

"You've only got forty minutes!" the man roared. "The Braves will be here any moment. Their trunks have just been delivered from the station!" He pointed at the door of the clubhouse. "Go inside and get to work!"

"Yes, sir!" said Jack and Annie.

Without another word, they hurried inside the visitors' clubhouse. And they got to work!

4

GOOD JOB, BOYS!

Jack and Annie knew exactly what to do. Jack felt like he'd been a batboy all his life. He hung his bag on a hook. Then he and Annie headed for the equipment trunks lined up near the door.

They started with a trunk labeled UNIFORMS. They opened the lid. They pulled out white jerseys with red letters that spelled BRAVES.

Together, they swiftly hung up all the uniforms in a row of lockers. They finished just as the Braves arrived.

All the men laughed and joked with each other as they spilled into the clubhouse. No one spoke to Jack or Annie, though. In fact, no one even looked at them.

Jack and Annie paid no attention to the team, either. Their magic caps helped them know the rules: *Batboys never bother the players. They never get in their way.*

Next Jack opened an equipment trunk labeled CLEATS & HELMETS. He and Annie pulled out baseball shoes and batting gear.

They used rags to wipe everything off. Then they quickly lined up the shoes on benches.

Jack and Annie hurried to a trunk labeled BATS. Together they pushed the trunk out of the visitors' clubhouse and toward the ball field.

"Yikes, look at the time!" said Annie. She pointed to a large clock over the scoreboard. "We only have twenty minutes till the game starts."

"And lots more to do!" said Jack. "Full speed!"

They pushed the trunk over to the visitors' dugout under the stands. Then, racing against the

clock, they flew through the rest of their tasks.

Jack quickly unloaded bats from the trunk. He handed them to Annie. She placed them on the shelves of a bat rack inside the dugout.

They rushed back to the visitors' clubhouse and unloaded another trunk. They pulled out a first-aid kit, shin guards, a catcher's mitt and mask, and boxes of chewing gum. They carried all these things to the Braves dugout.

By now, the home team, the Brooklyn Dodgers, had left the field. The visiting Boston Braves had started their warm-up. The noise in the ballpark was deafening. The stands were full.

"Hey, batboys!" a girl yelled.

"Get us an autographed ball!" a boy yelled.

Jack looked up. Kids were shouting at them from the stands.

"An autographed ball!"

"Please! Please!"

"Sorry!" yelled Annie.

Jack shook his head. They both knew the rule: *Batboys never do favors for fans.*

Jack and Annie hurried back into the club-house. They unloaded towels from a trunk. They filled jugs with water from a sink. They packed baseballs into a canvas bag. Then they carried everything to the dugout and put it in all the right places.

"Uniforms, cleats, shin guards, masks . . . ," said Annie.

"Water, first-aid kit, bats, towels, baseballs, chewing gum," said Jack. "Anything else?"

"Nope. We did it!" said Annie, looking at the clock. It was 2:25. The game would start in five minutes.

"Good job, boys!" said the clubhouse manager as he passed by.

"Thanks," said Annie.

Jack and Annie quickly took their seats on the bench in the dugout. The Boston Braves players sat near them, looking tense. Some scowled and folded their arms. Others chewed gum or tapped their feet.

A voice came over the loudspeaker: "Ladies and

gentlemen, please rise for the national anthem."

The crowd stood. The players stepped out of the dugout and placed their baseball caps over their hearts.

Oh, no! thought Jack. He and Annie couldn't take their caps off! If they did, everyone would see them as young kids—and see Annie as a girl!

Annie took Jack's arm. She pulled him back into a shadowy area inside the dugout. There, they placed only their hands over their hearts. Jack desperately hoped none of the players would turn around and notice them.

A man sang "The Star-Spangled Banner" in a deep, rich voice.

O say can you see,
By the dawn's early light,
What so proudly we hailed
At the twilight's last gleaming . . .

Jack nervously kept his eyes on the flag flapping in the breeze. *Hurry, hurry,* he thought.

Finally the singer sang the last lines:

O say does that star-spangled banner yet wave
O'er the land of the free
And the home of the brave?

The national anthem was over. The players all put their caps back on.

"Play ball!" roared an umpire at home plate.

"Whew," Jack said to Annie, and they stepped out from the dugout.

Noise filled the park—fans cheering, horns honking, bells clanging.

"See ya!" said Annie.

"Yep!" said Jack.

They both knew exactly what to do.

Annie was in charge of bats. She ran to the batting circle. She knelt on the ground, ready to pick up the bats the players dropped at home plate.

Jack was in charge of baseballs. He hauled the canvas bag over to a stool near the edge of the diamond. He sat down.

A strong breeze gusted over Ebbets Field. Jack pulled his cap down firmly on his head. Then he leaned forward to watch the game. His heart was racing.

Now the hard part begins, he thought.

5

FOUL BALL!

Jack kept an eagle eye on all the players. He watched the Dodgers take their positions on the field.

He watched the Braves batter choose a bat and head to home plate.

He watched the Dodgers pitcher wind up and throw.

The Braves batter hit the ball hard. It landed outside the foul line.

"Foul ball!" called the umpire.

Jack jumped up and ran to get the ball. He tossed it smoothly to the umpire at home plate. Then he returned to his stool.

Now and then the wind gusted through the ballpark. But each time, Jack grabbed his cap to make sure it stayed on his head.

The pitcher pitched another ball.

The batter swung his bat. He missed.

"Strike!"

The pitcher pitched again.

The batter hit a ground ball. He dropped his bat and ran toward first base.

The pitcher snatched up the ball and threw it. The first baseman caught it—just before the batter reached the base!

"Out!" called the first-base umpire.

The Dodgers fans cheered. The Braves fans booed.

Annie picked up the player's bat and returned it to the dugout.

Jack darted to home plate and gave new baseballs to the umpire.

As the game went on, Jack and Annie stayed in the center of the action. But they never got in the way.

Annie picked up bats that the players dropped and replaced them in the rack.

Jack kept a close eye on all the baseballs. He counted the ones that went into the stands. He raced after foul balls. He carried three balls to the umpire for every three lost.

Fans cheered and booed. If the musicians in the stands didn't agree with an umpire's call, they played "Three Blind Mice."

Finally the Braves had three outs. It was time for the Dodgers to bat. Now *their* batboys would look after the balls and bats.

Jack and Annie headed to the clubhouse to get more water and towels for their team.

"Hey, kid!" A Braves coach pointed at Jack. "Move down the line."

Jack understood perfectly. Holding on to his cap, he jogged out to center field.

Jack sat on a stool close to the stands. His job

now was to retrieve ground balls outside the foul lines.

Within minutes, a foul rolled into right field. Jack ran and grabbed it. He tossed it perfectly to a Dodgers batboy.

"Yes!" Jack said to himself. He couldn't wait to throw again. He sat back on his stool, pressed his cap down on his head, and waited eagerly for more ground balls.

But as the Dodgers kept batting, no more balls came Jack's way. For the first time, he had a moment to think.

Why did Morgan send us to this particular game? Jack wondered. *Why did she call it "a big day for baseball"? Why did Otis say it was a big day, too?* So far, the game was pretty ordinary, Jack thought. It was even a little boring.

Plus, how was being a batboy supposed to make him a great player? He had only thrown a couple of balls, and he wouldn't get to bat at all!

"Hey, batboy!" a kid called from the stands behind him.

More souvenir seekers, Jack thought.

"An autographed ball!" another kid yelled.

Jack ignored the kids' shouting. He refused to look over his shoulder.

"A Dodgers cap!" "A Braves cap!" "*Your* cap!"

The begging soon turned to heckling and booing.

"Go home!"

"Go back where you came from!"

What do they mean? thought Jack. *Can they tell I'm from Frog Creek?*

He tried to ignore all the shouting. But the hecklers sounded different now. Their voices had grown harsh and mean. They sounded like grown-ups, not kids.

"You don't belong here!"

"Throw him out, ump!"

Jack started to get angry. This was more than just annoying.

"Get out of here!" another heckler shouted.

Jack couldn't help it. He whirled around and yelled, "*You* get out of here!"

To his surprise, Jack saw that the hecklers weren't yelling at *him*—or even looking at him.

"Don't let him bat!" someone shouted.

"Throw him out!" said another.

They were shouting at the Dodgers player who was up at bat. Many in the stands were cheering for him. But these few were yelling really mean things.

Why? Jack looked around. The batter was the black player he'd seen earlier. He seemed to be the only black player in the game. *Is that why these people are yelling?* Jack wondered.

The batter hit a ground ball to third base.

The third baseman grabbed it. He threw it to first.

"Out!" the umpire shouted.

"That's right! Throw him out!" a woman shrieked.

Jack was stunned. He didn't understand. The player ignored the jeers and walked calmly back to the dugout. He held his head high.

Jack wished he could go talk to the player. He

wanted to say something kind and supportive.

Suddenly a new batter hit a ground ball to left field. It was outside the line.

"Foul!" the umpire shouted.

Jack ran to get the ball.

At the same time, a kid jumped over the wall of the stands. The kid ran to get the foul ball, too.

Jack got there first. But as he bent down to grab the ball, the wind blew his cap off. The other boy snatched Jack's cap from the grass and took off!

6
Go!

"Hey!" shouted Jack. "Give that back!"

Jack had to get his cap! But first he had to get rid of the ball he was holding.

A Dodgers batboy at home plate held up his glove.

Jack hurled the ball toward him. But his throw didn't go very far. It nearly hit the umpire at first base.

The umpire yelled at Jack. So did some fans.

Jack was in shock. He didn't know what to do.

He looked around for the kid who had stolen his cap, but the kid was gone.

The umpire shouted something to a security guard on the sidelines. The guard started toward Jack.

Jack began running along the outfield wall toward the dugout. He had to get Annie! They had to get out of the ballpark!

Jack didn't see Annie in the Braves dugout. So he dashed inside the clubhouse. He grabbed his bag and threw it over his shoulder. Then he looked around wildly.

No one was there.

"Annie!" Jack shouted. "Annie!"

"What?" she called back.

Jack tore around the corner. He found Annie filling water jugs in the kitchen area.

"We have to go!" Jack cried. "Some kid stole my cap! A security guard is after me!"

"Oh, no!" said Annie.

The door to the clubhouse banged open.

Annie rushed over to Jack. She pulled off her magic cap and placed it on his head. Then she hid behind the door.

The guard and the clubhouse manager came around the corner to the kitchen area.

"Hello, kid," the guard said, nodding at Jack. He was the same guard who'd brought them into the ballpark.

45

"Hello," said Jack. Annie's cap made him feel calm and confident again.

"Did you see a young boy come in here?" the guard asked.

"A young boy?" Jack asked.

"A skinny little guy wearing glasses," the guard said. "He was trespassing on the field."

"Oh. No, sir," said Jack, shaking his head. "I didn't see a skinny little guy."

"Okay." The guard turned to the clubhouse manager. "Let's check outside."

As they turned to go, the manager spied Annie behind the door.

"Hey! What are you doing in here, missy?" he said.

"I'm a batboy," said Annie.

"No, you're not! You're a little girl!" said the manager.

"You can't be in here!" shouted the guard. "We'll lose our jobs!"

"Wait!" said Jack. He pulled off the magic cap and tossed it to Annie.

She put it on and looked up. "See? I'm a bat-boy!" she said.

The clubhouse manager and the guard looked very confused. They squinted at Annie.

"Oh, I see that now," the manager grumbled. "Well, we'd better look outside."

But as the guard turned to Jack, he gasped. "Wait a minute! *You're* the little kid we're looking for!"

"No! He's not!" said Annie. "He's a batboy!" She pulled off the magic cap and tried to put it on Jack's head.

The guard snatched it away from her. "I'll take that!"

"I don't know what's going on here," said the manager, "but you kids have to get out—now!"

"Uh, can we take the water jugs to the guys first?" said Annie. "The team is thirsty."

"*NO!*" yelled the clubhouse manager and the guard together.

"March!" said the guard.

Jack and Annie headed for the door.

Outside the clubhouse, the security guard pointed toward the exit.

"That way!" he said.

Jack kept his head down as he walked with Annie. The two men followed them. Jack hoped no one was watching. When he heard laughter, he was sure people were laughing at them.

"Hurry up!" ordered the manager.

Jack and Annie stepped from the open park onto the ramp. They walked ahead of the guard and the manager through a turnstile. Then they headed into the huge round lobby.

Ticket sellers gawked at them as they crossed the room. The guard and the manager led them out through one of the doors.

Outside on the street, Annie stopped and looked at the manager. "Sir, remember—"

"Keep going!" the guard said.

"Remember when you said, 'Good job, boys'?" Annie said. "That was *us*."

The manager ignored her.

"Go!" he said. He pointed down the street. "And don't ever come anywhere near this ballpark again! Never again!"

7

SHORTCUT TO A GOOD PLACE

As Jack and Annie started down the sidewalk, the wind picked up. But the wind didn't matter anymore, Jack thought miserably.

"That wasn't fair," said Annie. "We worked hard."

"Who cares?" said Jack. He felt sick. A wonderful day had turned terrible. Morgan's plan was a big failure. They hadn't learned anything about being great baseball players.

"We can't just leave now," said Annie. "What about Morgan's rhyme? We have to give Fly Ball away—and we can't do that until we hear the final score."

Jack looked back. The guard and the manager were still watching them.

"Well, we can't stay here," he said. "Or anywhere near here. Come on."

They rounded the stadium at the corner of Sullivan Place and Bedford Avenue. At that moment, two kids were racing down Bedford. They bumped right into Jack and Annie.

"Ow! Oops!" the kids cried, nearly falling down on the pavement.

"Oh! Sorry!" said Jack.

"Olive! Otis!" said Annie.

"I can't believe it!" said Jack.

"Crashing into you by accident!" said Annie.

"No accident!" said Olive. "We came to look for you!"

"We saw you from under the gate!" said Otis.

"Jack changed before our eyes!" said Olive. "One minute he's tall! Then he's short! One minute he can throw the ball! The next, he can't!"

"One minute Andy's a big boy!" said Otis. "The next—he's a little girl!"

"Not that little!" said Annie.

The twins laughed so hard they nearly fell down again. Annie started laughing, too. Then Jack joined in—he couldn't help it.

"What happened to you?" said Olive.

"It's hard to explain," said Annie.

"Really hard," said Jack, still laughing.

"You changed like magic!" said Otis.

"You're right," said Jack. "Just leave it at that."

"What are you going to do now?" said Olive.

"I don't know," said Annie. "We can't stay around Ebbets Field. But we need to hear the final score."

"Oh! We know a good place to hear the game!" Olive said as she looked at Otis. "Don't we?"

"We sure do!" said Otis, as if he'd read his twin's mind.

"We promise you'll *hear* the final score there!" said Olive.

"Where?" said Jack.

"You'll see!" said Olive. "Hold hands while we cross the avenue!" She grabbed Jack's hand.

Otis grabbed Annie's hand. "Let's go, girl!" he said.

"You can call me Annie," said Annie.

"Come on, Annie girl!" said Otis.

The twins pulled Jack and Annie away from Ebbets Field. Crossing the avenue, they all dodged a streetcar and jumped onto the sidewalk.

"That was risky!" said Jack.

"That's how the Dodgers got their name!" said Otis. "Fans have to dodge streetcars to get to the ballpark!"

"Really?" said Jack. "I didn't know that."

"So where are you taking us?" asked Annie.

"To a good place to hear the game," said Otis.

"We know a shortcut," said Olive.

"Of course you do!" said Jack, grinning.

The twins led Jack and Annie down a street with a fish shop and a bakery. They passed a candy store and headed into a maze of alleys. They ran under clotheslines strung high between buildings.

Laundry flapped overhead in the spring breeze.

They passed some girls playing hopscotch.

"Hi, Olive! Hi, Otis!" the girls yelled.

Next, they passed old men playing cards.

"Hey, Olive! Hey, Otis!" the men called, waving.

Finally the twins led Jack and Annie through an alley and down a quiet block. They stopped in front of a small brick house.

"Here we are!" said Otis. "The Granny House!"

"The Granny House?" said Jack.

"This is where our grannies live," said Olive.

"Two regular grannies and one great-great-granny," said Otis.

"Plus two great-aunts," said Olive.

"Wow. You're so lucky," said Annie. "You get to visit all of them at the same house."

"Mama says they spoil us," said Otis. "They give us cookies and cakes. Best of all—they let us listen to their radio!"

"Come on in!" said Olive. She opened the door and led Jack and Annie into the Granny House.

8

SAFE!

The small house smelled of fresh-baked cookies and coffee. The loud sound of a radio came from a back room.

The twins led Jack and Annie down a hallway to the entrance of the kitchen.

A large radio sat on the kitchen table. Four women were sitting in chairs, listening to the ball game. They were listening so closely, they didn't seem to know that Jack, Annie, and the twins had joined them.

Jack heard the roar of the crowd and the band

playing on the radio. He heard the announcer say:

"Fifth inning! The score: Brooklyn Dodgers, one—Boston Braves, one. Number 42 steps to the plate."

"Come on, Jackie! We're with you!" one of the women yelled.

"Give us a homer, son!" said another.

Jack heard the sound of a loud crack.

"Number 42 hits the ball!" the radio announcer shouted.

"Culler catches the fly! Out! Throws to second base! Out!"

"Noooo!" the women shouted.

"Number 42 hit into a double play! Two outs!" the announcer said.

The women groaned. "I hope they don't fire him," one said.

Everyone kept listening intently. Jack heard "Out!" and "Safe!" from the radio. He heard the bat crack against the ball. He heard "Foul ball!" He heard the band play "Three Blind Mice."

Again, he wondered why this was such a big

day for baseball. Nothing important had happened during the whole game.

But the women in the kitchen seemed to hang on to the announcer's every word.

"He's up again!" one said.

"Knock it out of the park, Jackie!" said another.

"Go, Jackie!" said another.

"Hush! Hush!" another said.

The kitchen grew quiet. The women leaned forward. A couple of them whispered a prayer.

"Bottom of the seventh! The Brooklyn Dodgers

are behind! Braves, three—Dodgers, two! And number 42 raises his bat high," said the announcer.

"We're with you, son!" one woman said.

Jack heard the bat crack against the ball.

"Robinson bunts—the ball rolls up the first-base line!" the announcer said. *"Stanky to third!"*

The crowd roared.

"And 42 to second base!" the announcer said. *"Reiser up to bat!"*

"Bring our boy home!" one of the women cried.

Crack!

"Reiser hits the ball!" the announcer said. *"Stanky scores! Here comes 42! He rounds third base! He's headed for home!"*

"Yes! Yes!" the women in the room shouted.

"Go, Jackie! Go!" one said, clapping her hands.

"Safe!" the announcer yelled.

"Safe!" the women in the kitchen echoed. A couple of them burst into tears.

Jack turned to Annie. He was so confused. "What's the big deal?" he whispered.

"Jackie Robinson, number 42, scores!" the announcer said.

"Jackie Robinson!" whispered Annie.

"Oh, man . . . ," said Jack. Of course! Finally he understood. Jackie Robinson was the first black player allowed to play with white players in major-league baseball.

"It's official now," the announcer said. *"Jackie Robinson has made history!"*

The women all hugged each other and laughed. Otis and Olive jumped up and down and cheered.

For the first time, the women turned toward

the doorway. When they caught sight of Jack and Annie, they seemed surprised.

"Well, hello!" one of them said. "Who are you?"

"Jack and Annie," said Annie.

"Our new friends," said Otis. "They were batboys in the game today. At least for a while."

"Until the magic wore off," said Olive.

The women looked puzzled. One of them gave Jack and Annie a big smile.

"My goodness," she said. "You're the first white people ever to come inside our home."

"Really?" said Annie.

"Really," the woman said. "Welcome." She pointed at a plate of chocolate chip cookies. "Would you like some cookies?"

"Yes, thank you," said Annie.

"Thank you," said Jack. He and Annie and the twins each took a cookie.

"Have as many as you like," the woman said. Then she and the others turned back to the radio.

The Dodgers were in the lead now.

Jack, Annie, and the twins ate their delicious

chewy cookies as they listened to the final innings.

The radio announcer reported each play, until finally he shouted, *"And there you have it, ladies and gentlemen! Final score: Brooklyn Dodgers, five—Boston Braves, three!"*

Everyone in the kitchen clapped.

"The Dodgers have won this one," said the announcer. *"And Jackie Robinson has finished his first major-league game!"*

9

THE OLDEST FAN OF ALL

After he heard the final score, Jack smiled. "Okay. Now we know why this is a big day for baseball."

"Yep," said Annie. "And now it's time to give Fly Ball away." She pointed at the twins.

"Of course," he said.

He turned to Otis and Olive. "We have a special gift for you."

He took the ball from his bag and held it out to the twins.

"No thanks," said Olive. "You keep it. You deserve it more."

"We have lots of baseballs," said Otis.

"You do?" said Annie.

"Sure. We grab them when they fly over the wall of the ballpark," said Otis.

"They're all in here," said Olive. "Come look! We'll show you!"

Jack and Annie followed the twins into a shadowy room off the hallway. The room smelled of roses and lavender.

Otis switched on a lamp. A *really* old woman sat in a rocking chair. She seemed to be sleeping.

"See? There," whispered Olive. She pointed to a basket filled with baseballs.

"We keep them here in Granny Beck's room. We know they'll be safe with her," said Otis.

"Oh," said Jack. He and Annie glanced at the sleeping woman.

"She's our great-great-granny," whispered Olive.

"She's a hundred and one years old," whispered Otis. "She was born a slave."

"Do I hear some little children talking about

64

me?" the ancient-looking woman asked. She opened her eyes and smiled.

"Yes, Granny Beck," said Otis. "Sorry we woke you up."

"I was just resting my eyes, sweetheart," she said. "Who's that with you?"

"Our friends Jack and Annie," said Olive. "They were batboys at the Dodgers game today."

"Come closer, children," said the great-great-grandmother.

Jack and Annie moved closer to her rocker.

"Did you see Jackie Robinson today?" she asked in a whispery voice.

"Yes, ma'am," said Annie.

"Did the crowd cheer for him?" she said.

"Yes, ma'am," said Jack.

"All of them?" she asked.

Jack felt he couldn't lie to her. "No, ma'am. A few people didn't," he said. "They yelled mean things."

"I'm sorry to hear that," she said. "What did Jackie do?"

"He ignored them," said Jack.

"He held his head high," said Annie. "And he walked back to the dugout without saying a word."

"Of course he did. He kept his mind on the game," the old woman said. "He kept his dignity. He rose above what's mean and low."

That's a good way to describe it, thought Jack.

"He walked toward the good," she whispered. "Always keep your eyes on the good, children. And always keep your self-respect."

"Yes, ma'am," said Jack.

"Jack!" whispered Annie. "Look!"

Annie pointed at the baseball in Jack's hand. Writing was magically appearing on the white ball. The letters spelled:

Jackie Robinson

The twins stared at the ball in amazement. "You have a ball with Jackie Robinson's autograph!" Otis said.

"The ball with the name," Jack said to Annie.

Annie grinned and nodded. She took the ball from Jack and held it out to Granny Beck.

"This belongs to you," Annie said. She placed the ball in the old woman's bent hands.

"Thank you," Granny Beck whispered. She looked at the autograph. "I must be his oldest fan."

Jack remembered the last three lines of the message from Morgan:

Give the ball with the name
To the one who knows best
The rules of the game.

"You know the rules of the game," Jack said softly.

"Yes. I do," she said. The old woman wrapped her wrinkled hands around the baseball. Then she closed her eyes again.

Olive motioned to Jack and Annie. They followed her and Otis out to the hallway.

Annie smiled at the twins. "Your great-great-granny is . . . well, great!"

They all laughed.

"I'm afraid we have to leave now," said Jack.

"Thanks for coming over," said Olive.

"Wait, I have a question," said Annie. "Why are we the first white people to ever visit your house?"

Olive shrugged. "I guess you're the first ones who ever wanted to."

"That's so weird," said Annie.

"Not really, Annie," said Jack. "There was a lot of racism in the 1940s."

"*Was?*" said Otis.

"You mean *is*," said Olive.

"Yeah . . . *is*," Jack said softly.

"But Jackie Robinson's starting to change things!" said Otis.

"That's true," said Jack. "Well, thank you for everything. You two really helped us today."

"You sure did," said Annie. "And now can you tell us how to get back to the park?"

"Easy," said Otis. He led them out the front door. "Go to the corner, turn left, and go about six blocks."

"Great, thanks!" said Jack.

"Bye!" said Annie.

"Bye!" said Olive and Otis.

Jack and Annie ran to the corner and turned left. In the brisk air, they walked quickly up a

busy street until they came to the city park. They
headed to the open area where they'd first met the
twins. The big kids shooting marbles were gone.
The girls playing jacks were gone. The man singing in Spanish was gone, too.

Jack and Annie kept walking until they came
to the small grove of trees. They found the rope
ladder and hurried up.

Inside the tree house, Annie grabbed their
Pennsylvania book. She found the picture of the
Frog Creek woods.

"Ready?" she asked Jack.

"Knock it out of the park," said Jack.

Annie laughed. She pointed at the picture and
said, "I wish we could go there!"

The wind started to blow.

The tree house started to spin.

It spun faster and faster.

Then everything was still.

Absolutely still.

10

HOME RUN

Leaves rustled in the woods. Shadows danced on the floor of the tree house. No time at all had passed in Frog Creek.

"We're back," said Jack with a smile. He and Annie were wearing their own clothes again.

"I wish Otis and Olive lived in Frog Creek," said Annie.

"Me too," said Jack.

"They really knew how to get around," said Annie. "They knew all the shortcuts!"

"Yeah, Grandpa says in his time, kids did a lot

by themselves," said Jack. "It's different now."

"Unless you have a magic tree house," said Annie.

Jack laughed. "Can you believe we just saw Jackie Robinson play at Ebbets Field?" he said.

"Let's look him up," said Annie.

Jack reached into his backpack and pulled out HISTORY OF BASEBALL.

"Funny. Our whole trip, we never thought to *read* about baseball," said Annie.

"That's because we were too busy *living* it," said Jack.

He found the page about Jackie Robinson. He read aloud:

Jackie Robinson was the first African American to play major-league baseball in America. He played his first game with the Brooklyn Dodgers at Ebbets Field in Brooklyn, New York, on April 15, 1947.

"A big day for baseball," said Annie.

"Yep, a really big day," said Jack. He kept reading:

In 1947, Robinson was voted Rookie of the Year. And in 1955, he was a World Series champion.

"What's Rookie of the Year?" Annie asked.

"The best new player," said Jack. He read on:

Jackie Robinson was not just a great baseball player. He also showed heroic strength in the face of racism. "I'm not concerned with your liking or disliking me," he once said. "All I ask is that you

73

respect me as a human being." His talent and courage helped inspire the civil rights movement.

"That's so cool," whispered Jack. He closed the book. He took a deep breath. "Well, we'd better get going. We have a lot to do."

"We do?" said Annie.

"Yep." Jack pulled on his backpack. Then he followed Annie down the rope ladder.

A gentle breeze blew as they started walking through the woods. Sunlight streamed between the trees.

"You said we have a lot to do," said Annie. "Like what?"

"Like go to the ballpark and try out for the baseball team," said Jack.

"Seriously? You changed your mind?" said Annie.

"Sure," said Jack. "Why not?"

"I thought you were afraid kids might laugh at you," said Annie.

"I can live with that," said Jack. "You?"

"Sure," said Annie.

"We just need to try our best," said Jack.

"And keep our self-respect," said Annie.

"Yeah, if we don't make the team, we can sign up to be a batboy or a batgirl," said Jack.

"Or a manager," said Annie.

"Or use Mom's phone to take photos of the games," said Jack.

"Hey, what about making videos?" said Annie.

"That'd be fun," said Jack.

"*So* fun," said Annie.

"You know . . . Morgan didn't send us to Brooklyn to become great baseball players," said Jack.

"I know," said Annie. "She sent us there to learn how to be brave and keep going."

"Yep, the rules of the game," said Jack. They stepped out of the woods onto their sunlit street.

"Better hurry," said Jack.

"Home run!" said Annie.

She and Jack took off through the bright sunlight, running for home.

Turn the page for a sneak peek at

Magic Tree House® Fact Tracker

Baseball

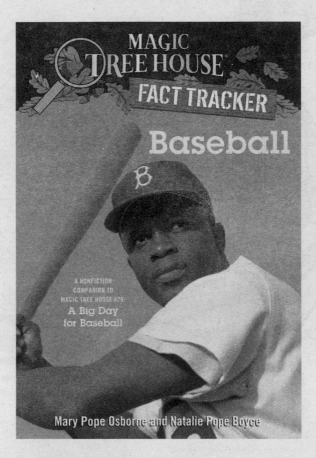

Positions on the Field

Right-handed batters usually hit to left field, so watch out! Needs to be fast and have great eyesight to judge where a ball will land.

Left fielder

Shortstop

Third baseman

Third base

Fields balls on the middle left side of the infield and covers second base when the second baseman is fielding the ball. More balls are hit to the shortstop than anyone else in the infield.

Covers third base and fields balls on the far left side of the infield. Needs a strong arm for the long throw to first base.

Pitcher

Home plate

Catcher

Catches pitches that batters don't hit. Has the best view of the field and shouts out advice to teammates.

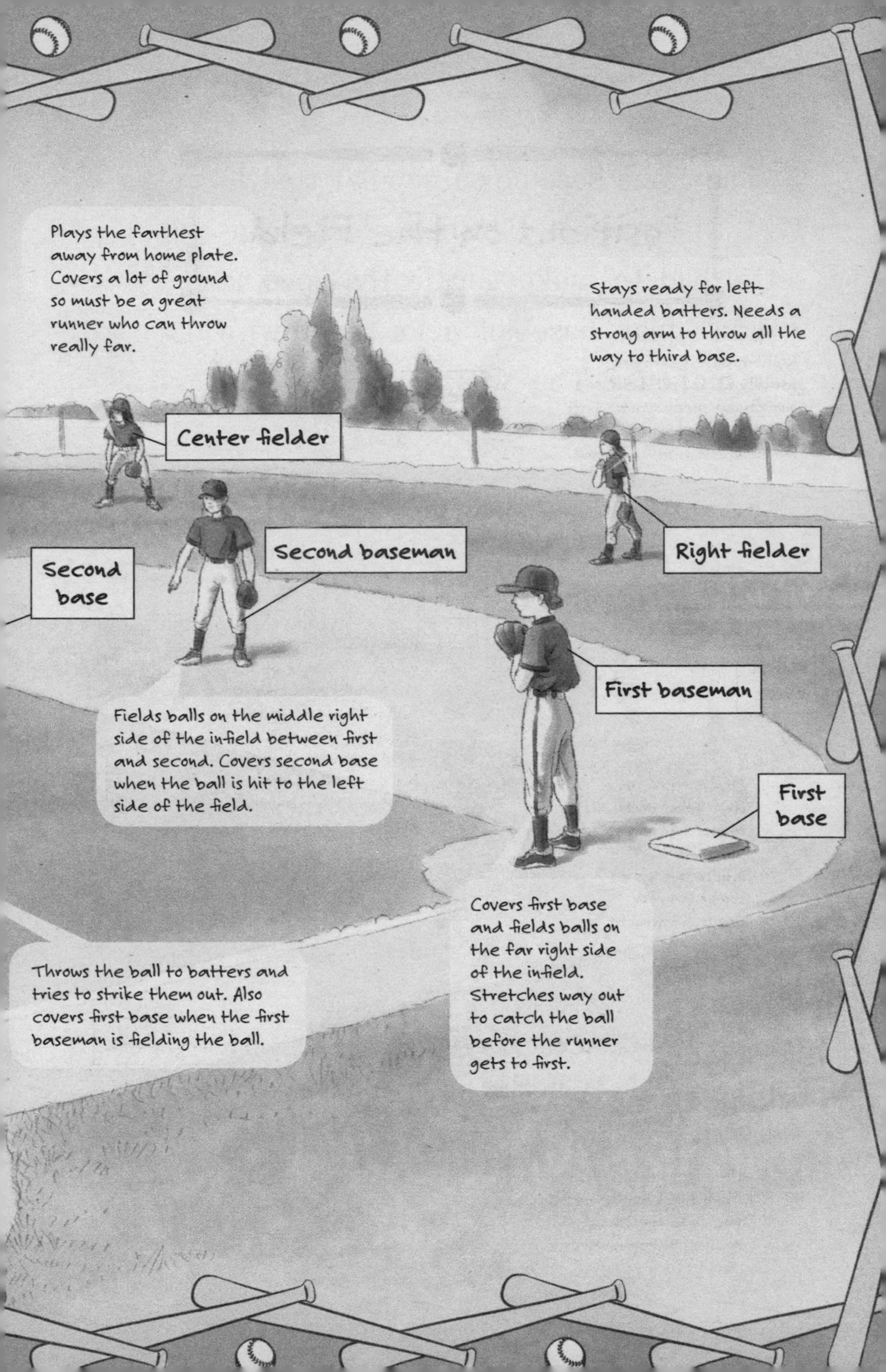

Plays the farthest away from home plate. Covers a lot of ground so must be a great runner who can throw really far.
Center fielder
Stays ready for left-handed batters. Needs a strong arm to throw all the way to third base.
Right fielder
Second base
Second baseman
First baseman
Fields balls on the middle right side of the infield between first and second. Covers second base when the ball is hit to the left side of the field.
First base
Covers first base and fields balls on the far right side of the infield. Stretches way out to catch the ball before the runner gets to first.
Throws the ball to batters and tries to strike them out. Also covers first base when the first baseman is fielding the ball.

The game became so popular that in 1791 the town of Pittsfield, Massachusetts, had to make a rule that people couldn't play baseball near the town's meetinghouse. This was to prevent broken windows.

Abraham Lincoln played baseball with his kids on the White House lawn!

Here's a special preview of

Magic Tree House® #30

HURRICANE HEROES IN TEXAS

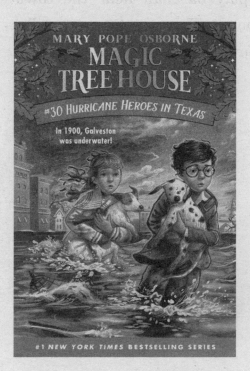

Jack and Annie must survive
the biggest storm of the century!

THE FLOOD

The giant waves slammed over the pier. They completely destroyed the bathhouses. Their broken wooden planks crashed into the sea.

The people on the beach screamed. They tried to flee from the incoming waves.

Jack and Annie ran with the crowd of people across the Strand to the boardwalk.

The surging waves rolled after them. Seawater swept over the beach and across the Strand. It covered the boardwalk and flooded the shops.

Jack and Annie began wading with the crowd

up 25th Street. The water was knee-deep and rising fast.

People rushed out of flooded stores and houses. They carried pets, children, and suitcases. They joined the others heading toward higher ground.

Jack saw a toddler slip from a man's shoulders into the churning seawater.

Jack grabbed the boy and pulled him out of the water.

"Thank you!" the boy's father cried. "Are you alone? Do you need help?"

"No thanks!" shouted Jack.

"Buddy! Bailey!" a girl screamed. Her two small dogs had slipped out of a basket.

Jack and Annie scooped up the dogs before the

water could sweep them away. They carried them back to the girl.

"Thank you!" she cried as they handed her the trembling dogs.

"Help!" someone yelled.

An old man was clinging to a lamppost, fighting the wind. Jack and Annie each put an arm around him. He pointed to a young woman, and Jack and Annie helped him wade through the water to her.

"Thank you!" the woman yelled. "Do you need help?"

"We're fine!" said Annie.

Jack and Annie forged on through the wind, rain, and rising seawater, helping anyone they could. Roof shingles and tiles flew off houses. Shutters flew off windows.

A fierce gust of wind knocked Jack and Annie over. They fell into the floodwater. They struggled to get back on their feet. They fell again. They got up again.

They used all their strength to keep moving. The street was like a river now. The seawater was above their waists—and still rising!

"Avenue L!" shouted Jack, pointing at a sign. "That's where the tree house is! It's a safe place to be for now."

"Okay!" said Annie. "We can climb up and figure out how to be more helpful."

As others kept moving up 25th Street, Jack and Annie turned onto Avenue L. The avenue was flooded now, too. They pushed past barrels, boards, and branches. Wreckage floated everywhere.

"There's the fence!" said Annie.

The top of the iron fence barely showed above the floodwater. The blue house was still standing. The tree house was still in the oak tree.

Jack and Annie hauled themselves over the iron fence and swam toward the oak. They grabbed low branches and clung to them. Jack looked around. The rope ladder was missing!

Magic Tree House®

#1: DINOSAURS BEFORE DARK
#2: THE KNIGHT AT DAWN
#3: MUMMIES IN THE MORNING
#4: PIRATES PAST NOON
#5: NIGHT OF THE NINJAS
#6: AFTERNOON ON THE AMAZON
#7: SUNSET OF THE SABERTOOTH
#8: MIDNIGHT ON THE MOON
#9: DOLPHINS AT DAYBREAK
#10: GHOST TOWN AT SUNDOWN
#11: LIONS AT LUNCHTIME
#12: POLAR BEARS PAST BEDTIME
#13: VACATION UNDER THE VOLCANO
#14: DAY OF THE DRAGON KING
#15: VIKING SHIPS AT SUNRISE
#16: HOUR OF THE OLYMPICS
#17: TONIGHT ON THE *TITANIC*
#18: BUFFALO BEFORE BREAKFAST
#19: TIGERS AT TWILIGHT
#20: DINGOES AT DINNERTIME
#21: CIVIL WAR ON SUNDAY
#22: REVOLUTIONARY WAR ON WEDNESDAY
#23: TWISTER ON TUESDAY
#24: EARTHQUAKE IN THE EARLY MORNING
#25: STAGE FRIGHT ON A SUMMER NIGHT
#26: GOOD MORNING, GORILLAS
#27: THANKSGIVING ON THURSDAY
#28: HIGH TIDE IN HAWAII
#29: A BIG DAY FOR BASEBALL
#30: HURRICANE HEROES IN TEXAS

Magic Tree House® Merlin Missions

#1: CHRISTMAS IN CAMELOT
#2: HAUNTED CASTLE ON HALLOWS EVE
#3: SUMMER OF THE SEA SERPENT
#4: WINTER OF THE ICE WIZARD
#5: CARNIVAL AT CANDLELIGHT
#6: SEASON OF THE SANDSTORMS
#7: NIGHT OF THE NEW MAGICIANS
#8: BLIZZARD OF THE BLUE MOON
#9: DRAGON OF THE RED DAWN
#10: MONDAY WITH A MAD GENIUS
#11: DARK DAY IN THE DEEP SEA
#12: EVE OF THE EMPEROR PENGUIN
#13: MOONLIGHT ON THE MAGIC FLUTE
#14: A GOOD NIGHT FOR GHOSTS
#15: LEPRECHAUN IN LATE WINTER
#16: A GHOST TALE FOR CHRISTMAS TIME
#17: A CRAZY DAY WITH COBRAS
#18: DOGS IN THE DEAD OF NIGHT
#19: ABE LINCOLN AT LAST!
#20: A PERFECT TIME FOR PANDAS
#21: STALLION BY STARLIGHT
#22: HURRY UP, HOUDINI!
#23: HIGH TIME FOR HEROES
#24: SOCCER ON SUNDAY
#25: SHADOW OF THE SHARK
#26: BALTO OF THE BLUE DAWN
#27: NIGHT OF THE NINTH DRAGON

Magic Tree House®
Super Editions

#1: WORLD AT WAR, 1944

Magic Tree House®
Fact Trackers

DINOSAURS

KNIGHTS AND CASTLES

MUMMIES AND PYRAMIDS

PIRATES

RAIN FORESTS

SPACE

TITANIC

TWISTERS AND OTHER TERRIBLE STORMS

DOLPHINS AND SHARKS

ANCIENT GREECE AND THE OLYMPICS

AMERICAN REVOLUTION

SABERTOOTHS AND THE ICE AGE

PILGRIMS

ANCIENT ROME AND POMPEII

TSUNAMIS AND OTHER NATURAL DISASTERS

POLAR BEARS AND THE ARCTIC

SEA MONSTERS

PENGUINS AND ANTARCTICA

LEONARDO DA VINCI

GHOSTS

LEPRECHAUNS AND IRISH FOLKLORE

RAGS AND RICHES: KIDS IN THE TIME OF
    CHARLES DICKENS

SNAKES AND OTHER REPTILES

DOG HEROES

ABRAHAM LINCOLN

PANDAS AND OTHER ENDANGERED SPECIES

HORSE HEROES

HEROES FOR ALL TIMES

SOCCER

NINJAS AND SAMURAI

CHINA: LAND OF THE EMPEROR'S GREAT
    WALL

SHARKS AND OTHER PREDATORS

VIKINGS

DOGSLEDDING AND EXTREME SPORTS

DRAGONS AND MYTHICAL CREATURES

WORLD WAR II

BASEBALL

WILD WEST

TEXAS

More Magic Tree House®

GAMES AND PUZZLES FROM THE TREE HOUSE

MAGIC TRICKS FROM THE TREE HOUSE

MY MAGIC TREE HOUSE JOURNAL

MAGIC TREE HOUSE SURVIVAL GUIDE

ANIMALS GAMES AND PUZZLES

MAGIC TREE HOUSE INCREDIBLE FACT BOOK